Litter Bug's HALLOWEEN

by Lydia M. Lacy

To Kamryn and Kourtney
Love Mommy

1

Litter Bug's Halloween

Copyright © 2006 Lydia M. Lacy

Published by G Publishing, LLC
P. O. Box 24374
Detroit, MI 48224

Illustrator: SOS Graphics and Designs

ISBN: 0-9788536-4-4

Library of Congress Control Number: 2006907746

Printed in the United States of America

It was Halloween! Litter Bug and his friends were very excited. Every year they would put on their favorite costumes and go Trick-o-Treating.

Litter Bug, Sam Snail, and Lady Bug would run up to every neighbor's porch and shout, "Trick-o-Treat, please give me something good to eat!"

Sam Snail and Lady Bug would put all of their treats in their bags. But not Litter Bug. He would rip open each snack and gobble it up throwing all of the wrappers down at each stop.

Lady Bug would say, "Litter Bug, don't litter on the streets, it is not nice."

But Litter Bug would respond smugly and say, "It is not my job to keep the streets clean."

Sam Snail yelled, "Litter Bug, pick that up! Those people worked very hard to keep their yard this nice."

But Litter Bug threw up his hands and responded, "It is not my job to keep their yard clean."

When the children reached the last house in their neighborhood, Lady Bug's bag was filled with treats. Sam Snail's pumpkin pail was filled with lots of goodies. Litter Bug's belly was filled too.

Knocking on the last door, Sam Snail shouted, "Trick-o-Treat, please give me something good to eat!"

This time the children received raisins and nuts.

"Yuck!" snapped Litter Bug, throwing the healthy snacks to the ground, "I don't want that and my stomach hurts. Let's go home."

Litter Bug saw the Halloween pumpkins, scarecrows, spider webs, and witches and he was scared.

Litter Bug began to cry. The other bugs were mad.

Sam Snail began to shout, "Look what you have done Litter Bug. Now we are lost and it is getting dark. Why did you drop all of those wrappers on the ground?"

"Shh!", said Lady Bug. "I hear something. I think it is a vampire."

Sam Snail said, "No, I hear it too. I think it is a witch."

"Wrong!" said Litter Bug. "It is my mom. I can smell her. "Mom. Over here mom. HELP!"

Slowly the mountain of trash began to move. Then, Litter Bug's mom appeared. "There you are."

"Mom, how did you find us?"

"I knew if I followed the trail of litter, I would find you."

The three bugs hugged Litter Bug's mom.

"I bought an extra bag for you, Litter Bug, to pick up all of the garbage you dropped along the way."

Looking up at his mom, Litter Bug pouted while retrieving the sack.

Turning to his friends, he pleaded, "Can you help me clean up this mess?"

Sam Snail and Lady Bug quickly responded, "No, it is not our job!"

Also by Lydia Lacy

Junk Food June

No More Miss B. Havin, a novel

Printed in the United States
65750LVS00002B